A Hug for you

David King

Illustrated by Rhiannon Archard

SANDYCOVE

an imprint of

PENGUIN BOOKS

For everyone who has missed a hug . . .
this book is for you

I am grateful to so many people who brought this wonderful story to life: to Lorraine, Patricia, Issy, Michael, Louise and all the team at Sandycove – thank you for your creativity, your wisdom and your support. To Rhiannon – thank you for breathing life into the story through your stunning illustrations. To Juelie and Willie – thank you for your vision, drive, commitment and genuine love for this project. To my wife, Fiona, and my children Danny, Katie, Robert, Adam and Sarah – I give you my unending thanks and love. Finally – to Adam – thank you for the hugs. D. K.

For Talitha, whose hugs brighten up my life every day. R. A.

SANYDCOVE
UK | USA | Canada | Ireland | Australia
India | New Zealand | South Africa

Sandycove is part of the Penguin Random House group of companies whose addresses can be found at global.penguinrandomhouse.com.

First published 2021
002

Text copyright © David King, 2021
Illustration copyright © Rhiannon Archard, 2021
Design and layout by Kazoo Independent Publishing Services Ltd.

The moral right of the copyright holders has been asserted

Printed in Italy by Graphicom

The authorized representative in the EEA is Penguin Random House Ireland, Morrison Chambers, 32 Nassau Street, Dublin D02 YH68

A CIP catalogue record for this book is available from the British Library

ISBN: 978–1–844–88585–5

www.greenpenguin.co.uk

Penguin Random House is committed to a sustainable future for our business, our readers and our planet. This book is made from Forest Stewardship Council® certified paper.

Nothing warms us up
    quite like a hug,
but what can we do when we
    can't be together?
This is the story of
    a new hug's adventure
and the boy who
    shared it with the world.

Adam is a joyful kid
who loves to go to school.

Every day he's learning more
and having fun with his friends, too.

But suddenly his class is inside a computer screen, with his friends
and adventures completely out of reach!
His teacher is working really hard to keep their learning going, so
Adam draws her a special gift to send across the distance . . .

I'm sending you this Virtual Hug
to say thanks for all you do.
We miss your classroom and the learning fun –
we promise we'll be back with you soon!

The teacher feels the hug wrap around her heart;
it is the boost of hope she needs.
She carries it with her everywhere –
but the hug's job is just beginning . . .

The teacher goes to the café, where people stand far apart,
wishing they could chat and play instead of just waving.
So many lonely faces . . . they could use a pick-me-up!
The teacher passes on the hug, and it gets right to work.

Let's send a hug in every cup to warm your heart and hands;
it will keep them snug until they can hold loved ones again.
With every sip remember that this isn't for much longer –
your friends will be waiting, and it'll be sweeter than hot chocolate.

A nurse brings the hug to the children's ward –
a place full of caring and kindness
where a little patient lies full of worry,
in need of some gentle comfort.

This hug is for you when you can't see our smiles,
to show they're still there, just hidden.
We hope you can see them instead in our eyes,
and they will hold you until you feel better.

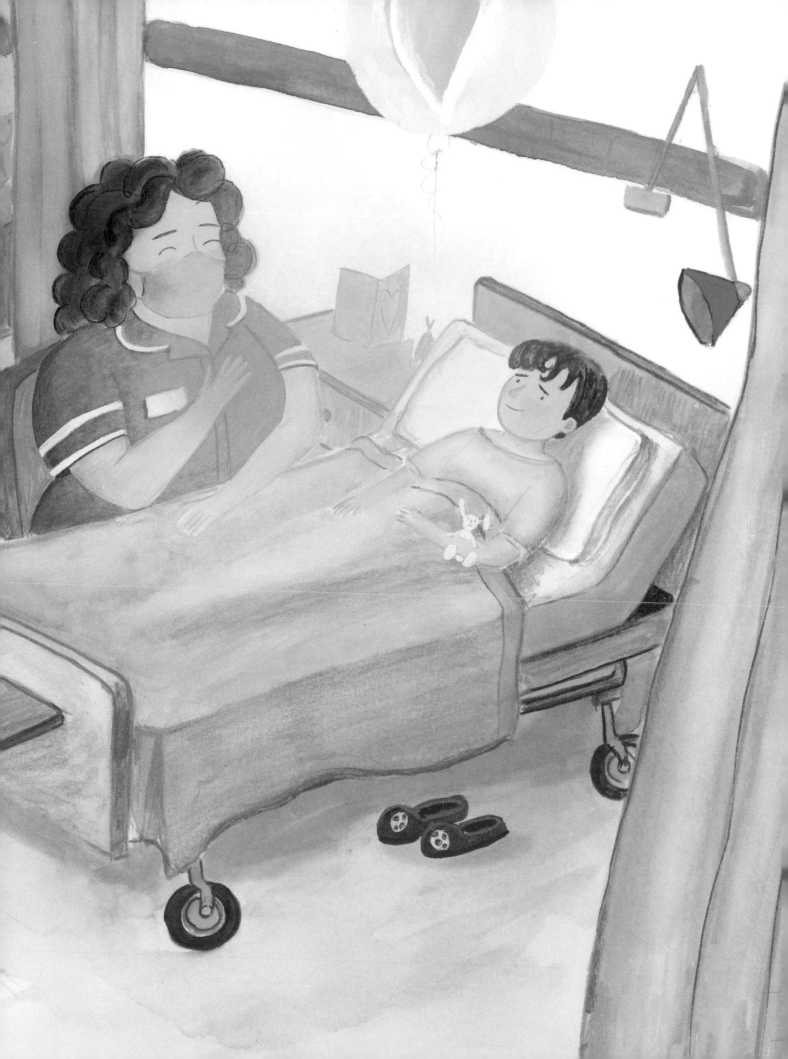

The patient heads home and wants nothing more
than to support his favourite team.
He adores the roar of the crowds, but instead
he's cheering alone at his television screen.

For every empty seat and silent game,
this hug will be there when we can't.
Win, lose or draw, even if you don't see us,
just know that we're all still behind you.

The captain wishes he could share his win
with the person who knows him best.
But his football-mad grandad is in isolation,
so he has to tell him through the window.

I wish you were there to see the whole thing,
but I felt your support from afar.
I'm sending this hug through the glass between us
so that you know I miss you and care.

Grandad waves his visitor goodbye
and finds himself in silence once more.
But the hug shines brightly all around him,
and he realizes it can go where he can't.

To my darling niece on opening night —
how I wish I could be there to see you shine!
Your talent is a gift to the entire world . . .
take this hug, and save a dance for me.

The dancer is feeling sad and worried –
when her group have all worked so hard,
the seats are empty with no cheers or applause,
But the show must still go on . . .

And so they dance just for each other,
and the hug joins in with them, too.
Ready for when the curtain rises again,
and lifts the group up with it.

The newest dancer is walking home
past closed shops and restaurants.
No one can stop for a smile and a chat —
it feels like her community is missing.

The hug sees its job is getting bigger,
so it grows large enough for everyone to see —
Your home is still here, and you're all here together,
I'll be a reminder when it gets hard to remember.

The hug keeps growing, bigger and brighter,
as everyone shares it around.
Soon it's a hug that wraps around the world,
and even the astronauts feel it!

Even though right now we feel far apart,
we've never been closer together.
The hug reminds us what's really important –
to send love to those who are near to our hearts.

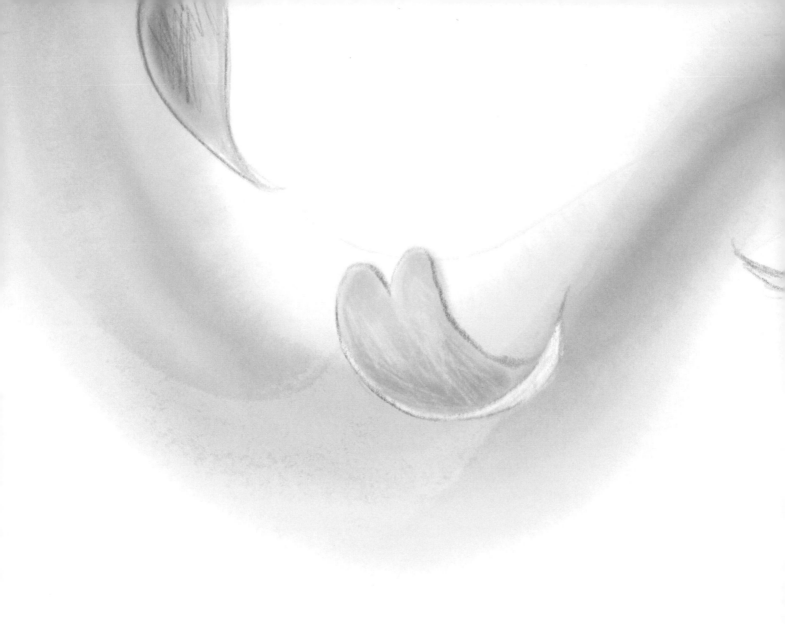

And sure enough, after it finishes
travelling around the world and beyond,
the hug comes home to the wonderful boy
who shared it first of all.

You're not done yet, the thoughtful lad says.
I need you to stay a bit longer.
Even when we can hug in person again,
we must remember to care for each other.

So Adam and the hug travel on together,
new adventures around every corner,
reminding us all of the power of hugs,
whether in person or across any distance.

*This book that you're holding and reading together
is a hug that you're sharing with love.
Never forget what we learned while apart —
and the power of one joyful heart.*

The Story of Adam's Virtual Hug

Adam is seven years old and lives with his family in County Cork, Ireland. He was born with a rare condition called osteogenesis imperfecta (OI) type III, which means that he has brittle bones and must be very careful when he moves around. He is a wheelchair user but can also take some steps.

Even though his condition means he does some things differently, nothing will stop Adam from achieving his many dreams!

Adam first drew the Virtual Hug for his teacher when he wasn't able to give her a real one during the Covid-19 pandemic. He showed it to her through the computer screen during virtual school, and it reminded them that even though they couldn't see each other in person, they were still connected.

After that, Adam brought the Virtual Hug to his regular hospital appointments and shared it with his doctors, nurses and care staff so he could still give them a hug – just in a different way.

In November 2020, Adam appeared on RTÉ's *The Late Late Toy Show™* – a famous Irish TV show that's broadcast every Christmas. He told the presenter about the Virtual Hug, and it touched the hearts of everyone watching because they were missing their families and friends, too.

During that programme, lots of people donated money for very important Irish children's charities and, with Adam's help, they raised over 6.5 million euro.

But that was only the start . . .

Since that night, the Virtual Hug has been used to connect people all over Ireland and the world during a time when we have had to stay apart. Suddenly, the Virtual Hug was being shared everywhere!

Turn over to see the real-life places the Virtual Hug has been used. Can you find them all in the book?

Where have you seen Adam's Virtual Hug?

Did you find Bubby on all of the pages, too?

Ireland's postal service, An Post, made Adam's Virtual Hug into a postmark, and it was stamped on every piece of post sent from Ireland at Christmas in 2020. This meant that there was an extra-special hug delivered with every letter.

Adam turned his Virtual Hug into a greeting card and, with the help of some wonderful Irish shops, raised over a quarter of a million euro for his two hospitals – Cork University Hospital and Children's Health Ireland at Temple Street, Dublin. Now everyone could send their own Virtual Hug to the loved ones they were missing in Ireland . . . and all around the world.

On the 21st January 2021, Adam's Virtual Hug was projected onto Irish landmarks all over the country for National Hugging Day. People were able to look at amazing buildings and monuments like the Samuel Beckett Bridge and remember that we were all working together to keep each other safe during the pandemic.

Every year on St Patrick's Day, the Irish Taoiseach (prime minister) and the American President have a meeting in the White House in Washington DC.

In 2021, because of Covid-19, they had to have a video call instead. The Taoiseach wore a gold pin of Adam's Virtual Hug to remind them of the important connection between Ireland and America. The President of the United States, Joe Biden, was so amazed by Adam's Virtual Hug that he wrote a letter to Adam, thanking him for spreading a message of love and connection around the world.

In June 2021, the hug made its way into space. A copy of Adam's Virtual Hug was sent into orbit as part of Virgin Galactic's Unity project and a video of it floating in zero gravity was beamed down to the world watching below. Who knows where we will see the hug next!